WE CAN READ!™

Little Honu

by Jacqueline Sweeney

photography by G. K. & Vikki Hart
photo illustration by Blind Mice Studio

BENCHMARK BOOKS

MARSHALL CAVENDISH
NEW YORK

For Matt, my Gus

With thanks to Daria Murphy, principal of Scotchtown
Elementary School, Goshen, New York,
and former reading specialist, for reading this
manuscript with care and for writing the
"We Can Read and Learn" activity guide.

Benchmark Books
Marshall Cavendish
99 White Plains Road
Tarrytown, New York 10591
www.marshallcavendish.com

Text copyright © 2003 by Jacqueline Sweeney
Photo illustrations © 2003 by G.K. & Vikki Hart
and Mark and Kendra Empey

Library of Congress Cataloging-in-Publication Data

Sweeney, Jacqueline.
Little Honu / by Jacqueline Sweeney ; photography by G.K. and Vikki
Hart ; photo illustration by Blind Mice Studio.
p. cm. -- (We can read!)
Summary: Gus, a turtle on a trip to Hawaii, becomes jealous of a sea turtle he
notices swimming in the ocean but in the end learns to accept that he is not the
kind of turtle that can swim very well.
ISBN 0-7614-1512-2
[1. Sea turtles--Fiction. 2. Turtles--Fiction. 3.
Self-acceptance--Fiction. 4. Hawaii--Fiction.] I. Hart, G. K., ill. II.
Hart, Vikki, ill. III. Title.
PZ7.S974255 Li 2003   [E]--dc21   2002003238

Printed in Italy

1 3 5 6 4 2

Characters

Eddie

Tim

Jim

Ron

Kono

Molly

Gus

Big Honu

Hildy

Ladybug

A letter!" yelled Eddie.

"It's from Gus!"

"Dear guys," he read,

"Here we are in Hawaii."

Eddie held up a picture.

...mber Sally's
...ono? He helped
...t of the box on the
...rst day.
We also met Big Honu.
He is a green sea turtle.

"Look at Molly's flower," said Tim.

"And Gus's hat!"

"Who's the little guy?" asked Ron.

"That's Kono the gecko,"
  said Eddie, "a new friend."

    "Who's the big guy?" asked Jim.

      "Big Honu," said Eddie.

        "Molly wrote a story

about him and Gus. Listen…"   7

One day in Hawaii
Kono was looking for Gus.
"He's watching the turtles,"
said Molly.
"Again?" said Kono.
"I wonder why."

Kono found Gus at the beach.

"You look sad," he said.
Gus pointed at a brown head
bobbing in the waves.

"I want to be his friend," he sighed,

"but I'm different."

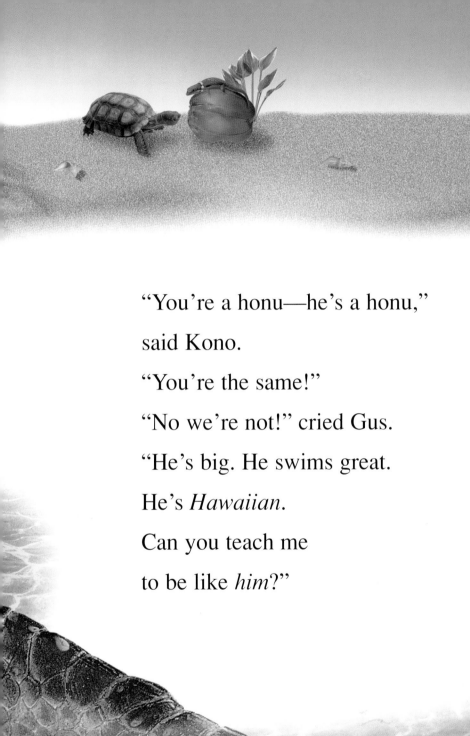

"You're a honu—he's a honu,"
said Kono.
"You're the same!"
"No we're not!" cried Gus.
"He's big. He swims great.
He's *Hawaiian.*
Can you teach me
to be like *him*?"

"I'll try," said Kono.

He plopped a gob of seaweed
in front of Gus.
"First you must eat limu," he said.
"Yuck!" cried Gus.

Kono sighed.
"We have to shop."

They shopped for shirts.

"More flowers!" chirped Kono.

They shopped for sunglasses
and hats.

Finally they went home.

When Molly saw Gus
she dropped a bowl
of poha.
Hildy stopped singing.
Ladybug flew into a wall.

"Time for the beach,"
chirped Kono.

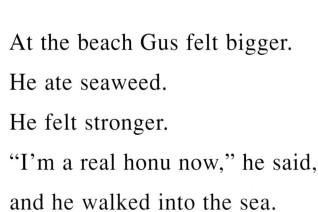

At the beach Gus felt bigger.

He ate seaweed.

He felt stronger.

"I'm a real honu now," he said,

and he walked into the sea.

The water was wild and stung
his eyes. Wave after wave
crashed on his head.
A huge wave rolled him
onto the beach.
Gus gasped
and tried again.

But something stopped him.

"Stay here, Little Honu,"

said a deep voice.

"You know you can't swim."

It was Big Honu!

Gus began to cry.

"Then how can we be friends?"

"Just be yourself," said the turtle.

"My legs work best in water.

Your legs work best on land.

So I'll meet you every morning

on the sand."

"After all, we are ohana,"
said Big Honu.
"We are family."

"Wait 'til the guys
at Willow Pond see this!"
said Gus.

WE CAN READ AND LEARN

The following activities, which complement *Little Honu*, are designed to help children build skills in vocabulary, phonics, critical thinking, and creative writing.

LITTLE HONU'S CHALLENGE WORDS

The Hawaiian alphabet has only twelve letters–five vowels (a, e, i, o, u) and seven consonants (h, k, l, m, n, p, w). The vowels are pronounced as follows: **a**–*ah* as in "father"; **e**–*eh* as in "bet"; **i**–*ee* as in "see"; **o**–*oh* as in "sole"; **u**–*oo* as in "moon". Help children pronounce the Hawaiian words that appear in *Little Honu*. Then discuss their meanings.

honu	poha	Kono	limu
Hawaii	ohana		

Help children figure out the meanings of the following English words by focusing on the contexts in *Little Honu* in which they appear.

gasped	picture	watching	stung
finally	wonder	pointed	bobbing
stronger	sighed	different	gob

FUN WITH PHONICS

Draw five turtles, cut them out, and attach them in a row to a wall or to a large piece of paper. Write a different vowel on the back of each, and above the five turtles write in big letters "Vowel Turtles." Explain that vowel turtles have a strange diet. They only eat words containing vowels followed immediately by the letter *r* (mention examples from the list below). A vowel turtle with an *a* on its back will only eat words that contain *ar*. A vowel turtle with an *e* on its back will only eat words that contain er. *I*, *o*, and *u* turtles follow suit. Vowel turtles have no problem finding words to eat. They do, however, have problems pronouncing the words they eat. They only know the long and short sounds that vowels make on their own. They don't know what vowels sound like when they are paired with *r*'s in words.

Help children teach the vowel turtles how to say the words they eat.

Write each word listed below on strips of green paper cut to look like limu (seaweed).

ar: **f**ar, **ar**e
er: aft**er**, lett**er**, flow**er**, diff**er**ent
ir: f**ir**st, sh**ir**t, ch**ir**p
or: f**or**, m**or**e
ur: pict**ur**e, t**ur**tle

Mix the strips up in a hat. Remove one strip and have children identify which turtle would eat it. Have them say aloud how the vowel in front of the *r* would sound on its own. Then have them say aloud the sound of the vowel and *r* pairing. Feed the appropriate vowel turtle the limu strip by taping it to its mouth. Repeat with each strip.

WISH YOU WERE HERE!

In this story, Gus sends a letter to his friends back at Willow Pond. Ask children to imagine being in Hawaii. Have them use plain white index cards to create postcards addressed to family members or classmates back home. On one side of the card they could draw Hawaiian scenes (sunsets, beaches, volcanoes). On the other they could write a message.

BIG HONU AND LITTLE HONU: OPPOSITE QUALITIES

Big Honu and Little Honu (Gus) have certain opposite qualities but it would be incorrect to talk about them as opposites. The ocean, which figures prominently in the story, has qualities opposite those of the land like wetness. But the ocean and the land are not opposites. Reinforce the concept by discussing opposites in the story such as up and down, light and dark, big and little, and near and far. Compare these examples with examples of things having opposite qualities, such as Big Honu and Little Honu, day and night, and ponds and oceans.

HAWAIIAN STYLE!

Children can make fun and brightly colored Hawaiian shirts by cutting shirt shapes from construction paper and decorating them with tropical prints and bright colors. Help children research the habitats and habits of different types of turtles. Children can record facts about the turtles on the backs of their shirts.

About the author

Jacqueline Sweeney is a poet and children's author. She has worked with children and teachers for over twenty-five years implementing writing workshops in schools throughout the United States. She specializes in motivating reluctant writers and shares her creative teaching methods in numerous professional books for teachers. Her most recent work includes the Benchmark Books series *Kids Express*, a series of anthologies of poetry and art by children, which she conceived of and edited. She lives in Catskill, New York.

About the photo illustrations

The photo illustrations are the collaborative effort of photographers G. K. and Vikki Hart and Mark and Kendra Empey of Blind Mice Studio. Following Mark Empey's sketched storyboard, G. K. and Vikki Hart photograph each animal and element individually. The images are then scanned and manipulated, pixel by pixel, by Mark and Kendra Empey at Blind Mice Studio. Each charming illustration may contain from 15 to 30 individual photographs.

All the animals that appear in this book were handled with love. They have been returned to or adopted by loving homes.

ER
SWE

Sweeney, Jacqueline
Little Honu

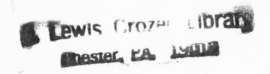